D0495852

Leon loves bugs – until he finds he is one!

Dyan Sheldon is a children's writer, adult novelist and humorist. Her children's titles include the award-winning *The Whales' Song*, as well as *Elena the Frog*; *Lizzie and Charley Go Shopping*; *Lizzie and Charley Go to the Movies*; *Lizzie and Charley Go Away for the Weekend*; *Undercover Angel*; *Undercover Angel Strikes Again* and *He's Not My Dog*. Among her numerous titles for young adults are *Confessions of a Teenage Drama Queen*; *My Perfect Life*; *The Boy of My Dreams*; *Planet Janet* and *Tall, Thin and Blonde*.

Scoular Anderson has illustrated over a hundred books including Judy Allen's *The Most Brilliant Trick Ever* and *A Puzzling Day at Castle MacPelican* and *MacPelican's American Adventure*, both of which he wrote himself. A keen walker and gardener, he lives in Argyll, Scotland.

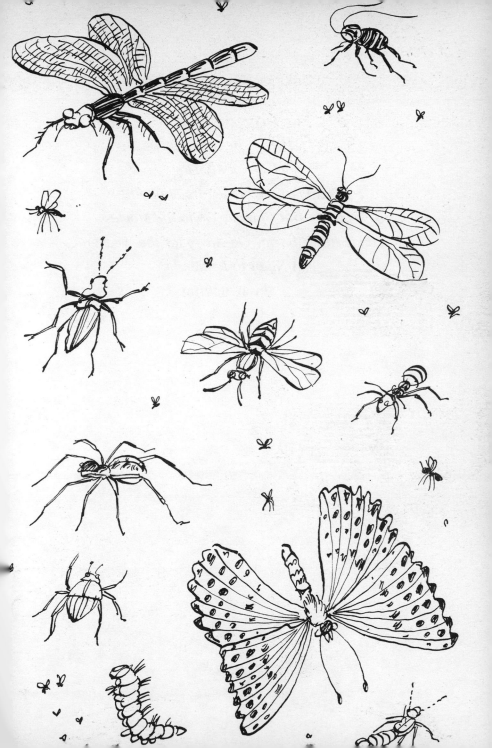

Books by the same author

Elena the Frog
Harry the Explorer
He's Not My Dog
Lizzie and Charley Go Shopping
Lizzie and Charley Go to the Movies
Lizzie and Charley Go Away for the Weekend
A Night to Remember
Sky Watching

DYAN SHELDON

Leon Loves Bugs

Illustrations by Scoular Anderson

WALKER BOOKS
AND SUBSIDIARIES
LONDON • BOSTON • SYDNEY

NORTHAMPTONSHIRE LIBRARIES	
BfS	23 JUN 2003
F	

First published 2000 by
Walker Books Ltd, 87 Vauxhall Walk
London SE11 5HJ

This edition published 2003

2 4 6 8 10 9 7 5 3 1

Text © 2000 Dyan Sheldon
Illustrations © 2000 Scoular Anderson

The right of Dyan Sheldon and Scoular Anderson to be
identified respectively as the author and illustrator of this
work has been asserted by them in accordance with
the Copyright, Designs and Patents Act 1988

This book has been typeset in Garamond

Printed in Great Britain by J.H. Haynes & Co. Ltd

All rights reserved. No part of this book may be reproduced,
transmitted or stored in an information retrieval system in any form
or by any means, graphic, electronic or mechanical, including
photocopying, taping and recording, without prior written
permission from the publisher.

British Library Cataloguing in Publication Data:
a catalogue record for this book is
available from the British Library

ISBN 0-7445-8328-4

CONTENTS

Leon Loved Bugs
9

Mrs Leary's Last Spider
15

Leon Lonely
20

Mrs Mittel's Surprise
24

Leon Thinks About Bugs
30

Only a Bug
36

Leon Loves Bugs
56

LEON LOVED BUGS

The children of Mrs Leary's third
year class stood around her in the
park, listening attentively to what
she was saying. That is, everyone
but Leon and Natasha were listening
attentively. Leon was dragging a
caterpillar backwards across the
ground. Natasha was watching him
out of the corner of her eye.

"Mrs Leary!" shouted Natasha. "Mrs Leary! Leon's playing with bugs again!"
Mrs Leary looked over the heads of the other children.

"Leon Mittel!" called Mrs Leary. "Whatever you're doing, stop it this minute!"

Leon stuck his tongue out at Natasha, then turned to Mrs Leary. "Me?" he asked innocently. "I'm not doing anything."

The rest of the class stepped aside as Mrs Leary marched towards Leon. Mrs Leary knew better than to believe that Leon wasn't doing *anything*. Leon Mittel was always doing something.

"What's that behind your back?" she demanded.

Leon dropped the dazed caterpillar on the grass.

"Nothing." He held up his hands.

 Mrs Leary frowned. If there was one thing she knew about Leon Mittel, it was that Leon Mittel loved bugs. They fascinated him. He could watch them for hours. Unfortunately, Leon didn't stop at watching. Mrs Leary had tried to encourage Leon to learn more about insects without actually harming them, but to no avail.

Knowing all of this, Mrs Leary was suspicious. But the caterpillar had vanished into the grass and Leon's hands were empty.

"I'm letting you off this time," said Mrs Leary sternly. "But remember that I'm watching you, Leon Mittel. Leave the bugs alone!"

Then Mrs Leary became involved in squirrels again, and forgot all about Leon.

Leon, however, didn't forget that Natasha had got him into trouble again. It was always Natasha and her big mouth who told on him. Leon decided that it was time to teach Natasha a lesson.

While the other children stared up into the branches at the leaping squirrels, Leon stood at the back. He pretended to be listening to Mrs Leary, too, but all the while he searched the ground for the perfect bug. At last he found it: a large black spider with tiny yellow dots on its back. Natasha hated spiders. Leon took an empty sweet box from his pocket and slipped the spider inside.

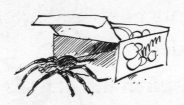

MRS LEARY'S LAST SPIDER

Leon waited all afternoon to get his revenge.

It wasn't until the last ten minutes of school that Mrs Leary finally turned her back on the class to write the week's spelling words on the board.

Every head in the class bent over its desk, copying the words from the board.

Every head, that was, except for
Leon's. His eyes on Mrs Leary,
Leon carefully removed the spider
from the box.

Natasha's head went up and
down as she looked
from the board to
her notebook.
Leon dropped
the spider down
the back of
Natasha's top as she started to
write the last word.

Natasha screamed.

By the time Mrs Leary had turned
round to see what was wrong,
Natasha was jumping up and down

in the aisle, shaking out her clothes.

"Get it off me!" she wailed.

The other girls started shrieking in sympathy.

The boys were shrieking, too, but they were shrieking with laughter.

The spider fell to the floor at Leon's feet.

"Leon Mittel!" Mrs Leary sailed down the aisle like a wasp with a mission. "Leon Mittel!" she boomed. "What did I tell you this morning about playing with bugs?"

"I wasn't playing with anything," protested Leon. He reached out one foot and squashed the panicking spider. "I don't know what Natasha's screaming about."

But Mrs Leary saw Leon's foot come down.

"Now look what you've done!"

Mrs Leary lifted Leon's trainer and removed the spider with two fingers.

"What's the big deal?" asked Leon. "It's only a spider."

"I'll show you what the big deal is," said Mrs Leary. "You've gone too far this time, Leon. From now on you'll stay in the office when the rest of the class goes to the park."

LEON LONELY

The weekly trip to the park was
Leon's favourite part of school, and
he missed it a lot.

While the other children were
looking for bird nests and rabbit
holes, Leon sat in the office
writing *I mustn't play with bugs* ...
a hundred times.

But the worst thing was that Mrs Leary sent a letter home and he wasn't allowed to play on his own in the garden any more.

Leon liked the garden even more than he liked the park. He usually spent his afternoons making clever traps for the bugs. On days when he was too lazy to set a trap, he would stomp on their homes or spray them with water. When he was in a bad mood, he might break off a leg or a wing.

The game Leon enjoyed most, however, was racing one bug against another. The winner won a gold star. There were fading gold stars scattered across the grass.

Now, however, Leon had to play in his room by himself.

Leon was lonely in his room.

"There's nothing to do," he grumbled.

"Nonsense," said Leon's mother. "Look at all the toys and games you have. There's plenty to do."

But Leon missed the bugs. Nothing seemed the same without them.

In the end, Leon decided that if he couldn't go to the insects, the insects would have to come to him.

MRS MITTEL'S SURPRISE

When his mother was safely busy
in another part of the house, Leon
snuck into the kitchen as silently as
a moth. Careful not to clank them
together, he took an armful of jars
from the recycling bin and scurried
back to his room.

While his mother vacuumed upstairs, Leon punched holes in all the jar lids with a nail.

By the time Mrs Mittel came back downstairs, he was sitting on the floor of his room doing a jigsaw of a butterfly.

"You see?" said his mother. "And you didn't think you'd find anything to do."

After that, Leon spent every afternoon waiting for the chance to gather bugs. Whenever his mother was busy with something else, he would go out into the garden with his jars.

Leon kept the jars filled with bugs under his bed when he wasn't at home.

As soon as he got
back from school,
he took them out
and played with
the bugs all
afternoon. When his mother called
him for supper, he put them back
in their hiding place. After supper
was over, he took them out again
until it was time to go to bed.

Mrs Mittel was delighted with the
way Leon was behaving. He stayed
in his room all the time, reading
and working on his jigsaw.

She was so pleased that she
decided to surprise him with a
book on bees.

Leon was in the middle of a water-
beetle race and didn't hear her knock.

"Leon!" called Mrs Mittel. "Leon,
I have something for you."

Leon still didn't look up. One of
the beetles was about to walk off the
edge of the desk.

He caught it just as his mother
stepped into the room.

"Leon—" said Mrs Mittel. The rest of her sentence died on her lips. There were jars of insects everywhere.

At last Mrs Mittel's eyes came to rest on Leon, who was staring back at her with a beetle in his hand.

"You've gone too far this time," she said. "Much too far."

Leon's mother made him return all the bugs to the garden.

"Maybe now you'll really think about bugs," she said, and she shut the door behind her with a bang.

Much too far.

LEON THINKS ABOUT BUGS

One lone cockchafer beetle
remained behind after Mrs Mittel
cleared the room.

Leon lay on his bed with the
beetle on the pillow beside him. For
a change, Leon was doing as he was
told. He was thinking about bugs.

The cockchafer beetle stared at
Leon from beneath its plume-like
antennae.

Leon stared back. He'd never
looked so closely or so quietly at an
insect before. For the first time he
thought about whether this was a
young beetle, or an old one. He
wondered whether it lived with
other beetles. He wondered
whether the other beetles wondered
where this beetle was.

Leon was still thinking about the
cockchafer beetle when he finally
fell asleep.

Leon woke up to a room bright
with sunshine.

He blinked in confusion and
rubbed his eyes. Something was
wrong. The bed was as big as the
school hall. The ceiling seemed
miles away.

Leon lifted himself on one elbow
and looked over the side of the bed.

He wasn't on the bed at all. He was on the pillow. The pillow was as big as the school hall; the bed was as big as a football pitch. The floor was so far below him that it made him dizzy just to look at it.

Leon crawled to the edge of the mattress. Clutching the blanket tightly, he leaned over. Leon's trainers looked as big as boats. Leon held his hands up in front of him. He stared at his feet. He, Leon Mittel, was the size of a cockchafer beetle.

Was this what happened when you thought too much about bugs?

Leon had to get help. He had to tell his mother.

Filled with fear, he shut his eyes and hurled himself off the bed.

Down … down … fell Leon.

Down …

down …

down…

ONLY A BUG

Leon landed on the pile of clothes that he'd left on the floor. He was winded, but unhurt.

He got to his feet as quickly as he could and headed for the door.

It took Leon several minutes just to get down from the pile of clothes.

Once he'd managed to roll down
the last hill of clothing, he had to
climb over his trainers.

Phew!

It was like scaling a mountain.
Then he had to get from the bed to
the door. The floor stretched before
him like a desert.

"I can't believe this," Leon
mumbled to himself as he struggled
across the carpet.

Every ball of fluff, every pencil, every pebble and every scrap of paper made him stop and start again.

"I never knew that being a bug was such hard work."

At last Leon stood in front of the bedroom door.

He looked up in dismay. The handle towered above his head.

"Oh, no!" cried Leon. "Now what do I do?"

Before he could answer his own question, Leon heard footsteps coming down the hall.

Oh, no!

"Get up, Leon!" shouted Leon's mother. "It's Saturday. We have things to do."

Leon flattened himself on the ground as the door swung open. His mother stepped on his foot as she walked into the room.

Leon screamed in agony and clutched his toes.

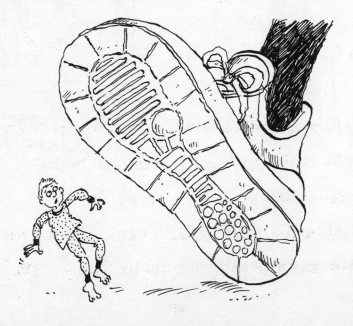

But Leon was no more than a bug now. His mother didn't hear his screams.

"Leon?" she said. "Leon, come out this minute. I must go to the shops."

Leon heaved himself on to one of his mother's trainers.

"Here!" he shouted. "I'm down here!"

But Leon's mother still didn't hear him.

"Suit yourself," she told the empty bed. "Hide and sulk if you want. I'm going to town."

And with that, she turned on her heel and marched back out of the room, taking Leon with her.

Leon didn't really enjoy riding on his mother's shoe. The heavy pounding of her foot gave him a headache. The speed at which she moved made him dizzy.

Leon clung to his mother's laces for dear life. Now that he was the size of a cockchafer beetle, there were dangers all around.

It was a blade of grass by the front gate that finally knocked Leon from his mother's shoe.

He struggled to his feet. The grass was as tall as trees.

"Mum!" gasped Leon. "Mum, I'm down here!"

I'm down here!

Without so much as a glance in his direction, Leon's mother thudded down the road towards the bus stop.

"Wait for me!" shouted Leon. "Wait for me!"

The bus stop was only a few metres from Leon's house, but if you were the size of a cockchafer beetle it might as well have been kilometres.

Leon took a deep breath and scuttled after his mother.

Everywhere he looked there were enormous feet. No one noticed bugs,

so Leon had to pay attention to avoid being stepped on.

Leon used to think it was funny to shove ants and beetles into the cracks in the pavement, but he didn't think it was funny now. He had to be careful not to get stuck in the cracks that, to him, were deep as ravines.

Sweating and panting, Leon reached the stop as the bus pulled in.

"Mum!" screamed Leon. "Mum, look down here!"

Leon's mother moved towards the bus.

Leon grabbed on to the hem of her skirt. Still hanging from the skirt, he bounced up the stairs and was dragged to a seat at the front.

He felt exhausted, but happy.
Now that they were on the bus, he
could catch his mother's attention.

He scratched at her leg to make
her look down.

Leon's mother didn't
look. She reached
down and flicked
him across the aisle.
He landed on his back
in an empty sweet
wrapper. Melted bits of chocolate
held him like glue. Leon's arms and
legs waved helplessly in the air.

The bus pulled out into the road. Leon had never noticed how much it shuddered before. It rocked him back and forth like an angry sea. It rocked so much that, as they took a sharp turn, it finally rocked him free.

Leon skidded across the aisle, and straight into a pool of lemonade that had been spilled on the floor.

"Help!" he screamed. "Help, I'm drowning!"

His mother didn't hear him, and nor did anyone else.

Leon paddled through the sticky liquid until he reached the toe of his mother's trainer. Panting and spluttering, he crawled up his mother's foot.

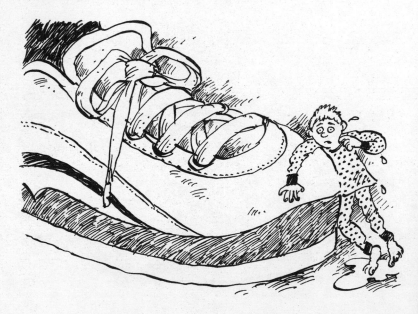

He grabbed hold of her skirt and slowly pulled himself up to her knees.

His mother's lap spread before him like an ocean.

Taking a deep breath, Leon moved across it.

Dizzy with relief, he got to his
feet and grabbed her finger.

"Mum!" shouted Leon. "Mum,
look! It's me!"

At last his mother looked.

"What's that?" she screamed.
"Another bug?"

In horror, he watched her raise
her hand to squash what she
thought was just another bug.

"Don't!" shrieked Leon. "Don't!
It's me!"

Her hand came down on him
like a lid…

LEON LOVES BUGS

Leon woke up with the sun streaming across his bed. He was still trembling from his dream.

Leon sat up slowly and looked around. Nothing had changed. His books and toys were still on the shelves. His trainers and dirty clothes were still at the side of the bed. The floor and the walls and the ceiling were all where they should be.

Leon's eyes fell on the solitary cockchafer beetle that was still on his pillow.

As he stared at the tiny bug, Leon realized that one thing had changed. For the first time in his life Leon had no desire to play with the beetle. He remembered how large everything had seemed in his dream. He remembered how frightened he'd been.

The cockchafer beetle must be frightened, too. It must want to be back in the oak tree the way Leon had wanted to be back in his bed.

Leon jumped up and put on his slippers. Very very gently, he picked up the beetle and raced outside.

Very very carefully,
Leon put the
cockchafer beetle
back on the leaf
where he'd found
it the day before.
As soon as it was
back in the tree, the
cockchafer opened its
wings. It brushed
Leon's cheek as it
flew away.

Leon smiled.
"I love bugs!"
Leon shouted to
the garden. "I
really, really do…"

I love bugs!

That afternoon, Leon sat in the garden until it was dark, reading the book his mother had bought him about bees.

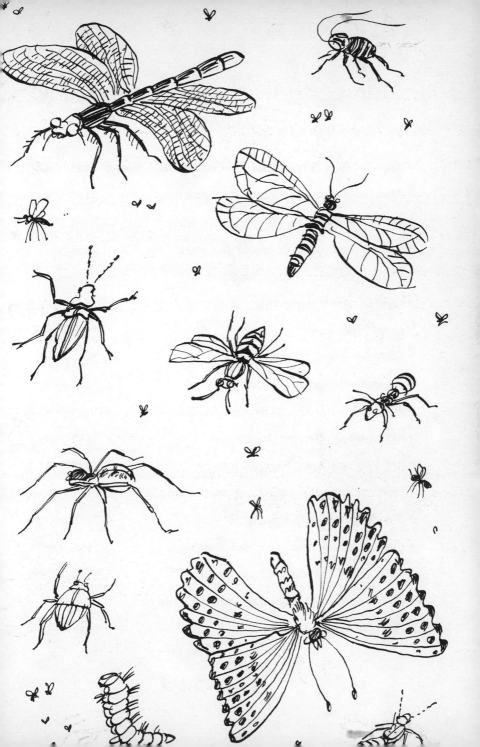

More *SPRINTERS* for you to enjoy!

- *Captain Abdul's Pirate School* Colin McNaughton 0-7445-5242-7
- *The Ghost in Annie's Room* Philippa Pearce 0-7445-5993-6
- *Molly and the Beanstalk* Pippa Goodhart 0-7445-5981-2
- *Taking the Cat's Way Home* Jan Mark 0-7445-8268-7
- *The Finger-eater* Dick King-Smith 0-7445-8269-5
- *Care of Henry* Anne Fine 0-7445-8270-9
- *Cup Final Kid* Martin Waddell 0-7445-8297-0
- *Lady Long-legs* Jan Mark 0-7445-8296-2
- *Patrick's Perfect Pet* Annalena McAfee 0-7445-8911-8
- *Me and My Big Mouse* Simon Cheshire 0-7445-5982-0
- *No Tights for George!* June Crebbin 0-7445-5999-5
- *Art, You're Magic!* Sam McBratney 0-7445-8985-1
- *Ernie and the Fishface Gang* Martin Waddell 0-7445-7868-X
- *Elena the Frog* Dyan Sheldon 0-7445-8960-6
- *Cool as a Cucumber* Michael Morpurgo 0-7445-9099-X
- *Little Stupendo Rides Again* Jon Blake 0-7445-9051-5
- *Tricky Nelly's Birthday Treat* Berlie Doherty 0-7445-9083-3
- *Fighting Dragons* Colin West 0-7445-8346-2

All at £3.99